After HAPPILY —EVER— AFTER

Goldilocks and the Just Right Club

After Happily Ever After was published in the United States
in 2009 and 2014 by Stone Arch Books, A Capstone Imprint
1710 Roe Crest Drive, North Mankato, Minnesota 56003
www.capstoneyoungreaders.com

First published by Orchard Books, a division of Hachette Children's Books
338 Euston Road, London NW1 3BH, United Kingdom

Library of Congress Cataloging-in-Publication Data is available
on the Library of Congress website.

ISBN: 978-1-4342-7963-7 (paperback)

Summary: After her adventure at the Three Bears' house, Goldilocks starts
a new school. She tries to fit in, but she's not a princess, a troll, or a ninja.
Goldilocks wants a group of friends who are just right for her, but that's
not so easy to find.

Designer: Russell Griesmer
Photo Credits: ShutterStock/Maaike Boot, 5, 6, 7, 52, 53

Printed in China.
092013   007737LEOS14

After HAPPILY -EVER- AFTER

Goldilocks and the Just Right Club

by Tony Bradman
illustrated by Sarah Warburton

STONE ARCH BOOKS®
a capstone imprint

TABLE OF CONTENTS

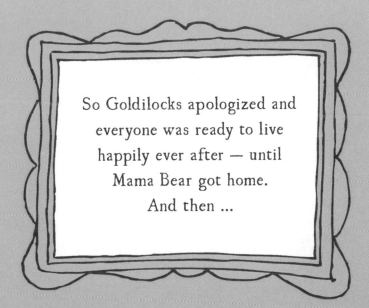

So Goldilocks apologized and
everyone was ready to live
happily ever after — until
Mama Bear got home.
And then ...

CHAPTER ONE

Goldilocks felt sick as they came around the corner and she saw her house. Mom and Dad were going to be seriously unhappy.

After all, she was being marched home
by an angry grown-up. And judging by the
frown on Mrs. Bear's face as she knocked
on the front door, she was still very angry.

"Goldilocks, sweetheart, where have you been?" asked Mom.

"Hi there," said Dad, noticing Mrs. Bear. "Who are you?"

"Mrs. Bear," she said. "Your daughter broke into our cottage."

"She did WHAT?" said Dad, horrified.
"Is this true, young lady?"

Goldilocks glanced up at him, nodded,
and burst into tears.

Mrs. Bear told Mom and Dad the whole
story. Soon they were frowning, too.

Mom and Dad said they were sorry.
They couldn't understand it because
Goldilocks was a good girl, and they
would pay for the damage.

Goldilocks said she was sorry, too.
Mrs. Bear seemed satisfied with that,
although she still looked pretty stern and
grumpy when she left. Goldilocks was
glad to see her go.

"I bet it was some kind of silly dare,"
Mom said. "You were with a group
of friends, someone suggested it, and
things got out of hand."

"No, Mom," said Goldilocks between sniffs. "I did it on my own."

Goldilocks would have loved to be part of a group of friends at school. But she'd never found the right group and she didn't know why.

Earlier that day, she'd felt very unhappy about it. That's why she went off into the woods after school instead of coming straight home.

And the Bears' cottage had been very tempting.

She knew she'd been very naughty. But climbing trees and splashing in muddy streams had been a lot of fun.

Trying on Mrs. Bear's clothes and playing with her makeup had been cool too.

"You're not unhappy at school, are you?" asked Dad.

Goldilocks didn't answer. Mom and Dad looked at each other and raised their eyebrows.

By the end of the week, they arranged for her to transfer to a new school.

CHAPTER TWO

Goldilocks was surprised, but pleased.
It might be a chance for her to find
some friends at last.

She felt excited when she said goodbye
to her parents and walked into her
school. But she was nervous, too.

"Settle down everybody," said Miss
Sweet, her new teacher. The children
were silent. "I'd like to introduce you
to Goldilocks, your new classmate. I'm
sure you'll do your best to make her feel
welcome."

Goldilocks smiled shyly. Thirty pairs of eyes stared back at her, but nobody spoke. Miss Sweet made the whole class say hello.

"Don't worry, dear," she whispered to Goldilocks. "Just be yourself, and I'm sure you'll fit right in."

At recess, Goldilocks stood in the playground watching everyone.

"Hi," a smiling girl said. "I'm Little Red Riding Hood, and this is Baby Bear. We were wondering if you'd like to play with us."

"Actually, we've met before — in my bedroom," Baby Bear said. "It was all very confusing, so you probably don't remember me."

"We like to play pretending games, don't we?" said Little Red Riding Hood. "Today we're deadly ninja warriors on a special mission."

"Thanks," said Goldilocks. "But no thanks."

Little Red Riding Hood and Baby Bear looked disappointed and walked off.

Little Red Riding Hood seems pretty cool, thought Goldilocks. But if she made friends with Baby Bear, she might have to meet scary Mrs. Bear again.

Besides, she had decided on the group
for her — the Princesses. That's what
she called them, anyway.

Their names were Maisy, Daisy, Molly, Polly, and Scarlett. They were the prettiest, most fashionable girls in the class.

They spent every recess brushing each other's hair and talking about clothes. Goldilocks thought they'd be just right.

And they were for a while. But after
a couple of days she began to feel that
something was wrong. She liked being
girly, but now she realized she could get
very bored with it too.

Then one morning it poured rain, and at lunchtime, the playground was covered with puddles. Goldilocks couldn't resist jumping in them and getting wet and muddy, and soon she was having lots of fun. But the Princesses were not impressed.

"She's not our kind of person after all. Let's go, girls," said Scarlett with her nose in the air, and the five of them turned their backs on Goldilocks.

Goldilocks was upset, but then she thought that maybe it was a good thing.

CHAPTER THREE

So the next day she stood in the playground watching everyone again. Soon Little Red Riding Hood and Baby Bear came up to her.

"Hey, would you like to jump rope with us?" said Baby Bear.

"You must be joking," Goldilocks muttered. She still felt the same about Baby Bear, and she thought they'd stop pestering her if she wasn't nice.

Besides, she had already found another group she liked.

She called them the Troll Boys. Their names were Benny, Lenny, Harry, Barry, and Jake. They were the loudest boys in her class.

They spent every recess running around making as much noise as they could. Goldilocks thought they would be just right.

And they were for a while. But soon
she got the same feeling as before.
Something about this was wrong, too.

She enjoyed being one of the boys.
But now she realized she could get very
bored with it as well.

Then one day, the Troll Boys decided they were going to have a burping contest. They thought it was hilarious, but Goldilocks didn't.

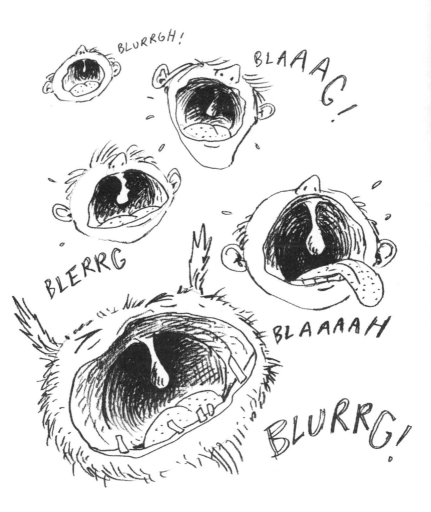

"Ugh, that's disgusting," she said. "Count me out."

"Suit yourself," Jake said rudely. "Come on guys, she probably wants to brush her hair." And the five of them turned their backs on her.

CHAPTER FOUR

That evening, Goldilocks hung out in her bedroom feeling sad. She was starting to think she would never be part of a group of friends.

"Just be yourself," Miss Sweet had said. But how could she do that? Girls didn't seem to like one side of her, and boys didn't seem to like the other.

That was why she had never fit in at her old school, and why her afternoon in the woods had been so much fun.

She'd been adventurous in the woods
and girly in the Bears' cottage, all in
the same day. Maybe she needed some
friends who liked both sides of her.

Suddenly she thought of Little Red
Riding Hood and Baby Bear. Little
Red Riding Hood had talked about
pretending to be a deadly ninja warrior.

Baby Bear had asked her to jump rope. They didn't seem to mind what they played as long as they had fun! They would be the perfect group for Goldilocks. She would just have to take the risk of meeting Mrs. Bear again.

So the next day at recess, Goldilocks
went straight up to Little Red Riding Hood
and Baby Bear and asked if she could
play with them.

"Although I'd understand if you didn't want anything to do with me," she said nervously. "I mean, I know I wasn't very nice to you before."

"Really?" said Little Red Riding Hood, puzzled. "I didn't notice." Then she smiled, and so did Baby Bear, and they all went off together.

Goldilocks really enjoyed spending time with her new friends. Little Red Riding Hood liked doing girly stuff, but she had an adventurous side as well. After all, she did do karate.

And Baby Bear was a real boy, but he didn't mind playing house or holding one end of a jump rope.

And once she got to know Goldilocks better, Mrs. Bear turned out to be friendly. Although she always kept a careful eye on things.

The only problem Goldilocks had was trying to choose a name for the three of them. Then it came to her.

They weren't too girly or too rough —
they were The Just Right Club. So
Goldilocks (and Mom and Dad, when
they got her report card) lived happily
ever after!

ABOUT THE AUTHOR

Tony Bradman writes for children of all ages. He is particularly well known for his top-selling Dilly the Dinosaur series. His other titles include the Happily Ever After series, *The Orchard Book of Heroes and Villains*, and *The Orchard Book of Swords*, *Sorcerers*, and *Superheroes*. Tony lives in South East London.

ABOUT THE ILLUSTRATOR

Sarah Warburton is a rising star in children's books. She is the llustrator of the Rumblewick series, which has been very well received at an international level. The series spans across both picture books and fiction. She has also illustrated nonfiction titles and the Happily Ever After series. She lives in Bristol, England, with her young baby and husband.